9/08

The Rottenest
Angel

Look for these
ROTTEN SCHOOL
books, too!

ROTTEN SCHOOL

GROWTH · LEARNING · PIZZA!

The Rottenest Angel

R.L. STINE

Illustrations by Trip Park

HarperCollins*Publishers*

A Parachute Press Book

For Noble
–TP

Library of Congress Cataloging-in-Publication Data is available.
ISBN-10: 0-06-078827-5 (trade bdg.) — ISBN-10: 0-06-078828-3 (lib. bdg.)
ISBN-13: 978-0-06-078827-8 (trade bdg.) — ISBN-13: 978-0-06-078828-5 (lib. bdg.)

Cover and interior design by mjcdesign
1 2 3 4 5 6 7 8 9 10
❖
First Edition

CONTENTS

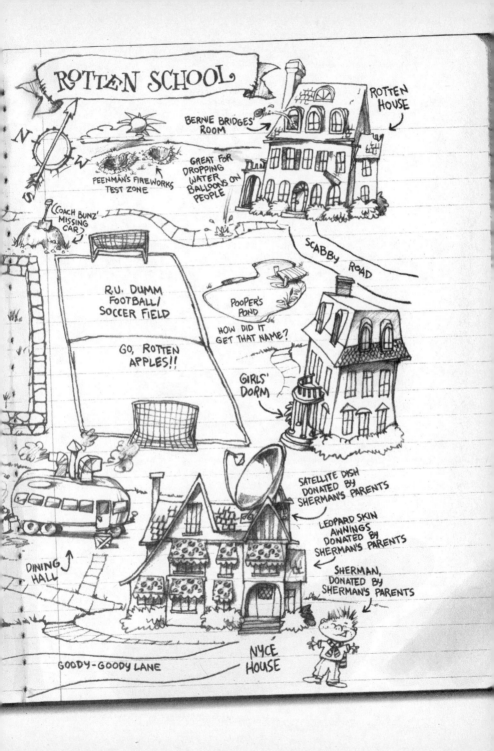

Good morning, Rotten Students. This is Headmaster Upchuck wishing everyone a Rotten Day. Here are this morning's important announcements....

Congratulations to the volunteers in Mr. Boring's Science class for proving that it is possible to rub the skin off your butt by sliding down the banister.

Ms. Sally Monella announces that the annual Spring Rain Festival has been canceled due to rain.

For a long time, our second-grade choir has been unhappy with its name—the Whining Wusses. The choir has finally found a new name. The kids voted to call themselves the Stone-Faced Zombie Cannibals.

An announcement from the Dining Hall. Chef Baloney *knows* there are fleas in the mashed potatoes. He'd like to tell all the students that it's okay to remove them with your fingers.

And finally, Coach Manley Bunz wants to remind the stupid idiots on the soccer team that it's bad sportsmanship to call people names.

Chapter 1

"HOW YOU DOIN'?"

A beautiful morning at Rotten School. The apple trees shimmered in the morning sunlight. The grass on the Great Lawn still sparkled with dew.

I strolled happily, singing the Rotten School Song to myself:

"Rah, rah, Rotten School!
I'd rather be in Rotten School—
Than NOT in school!"

It was Saturday, and I—Bernie Bridges—didn't

have a care in the world. Did I know that BIG trouble—with a capital BIG—was just minutes away? No with a capital NO.

"Dudes! Wait for Bernie B.!" I shouted. I waved to my three buddies and ran to catch up with them. Feenman and Crench had one of Belzer's shoes. They were tossing it back and forth, playing keep-away. Fun-loving dudes!

"How you doin'?" I asked.

"How YOU doin'?" Feenman replied.

"How YOU doin'?" Belzer asked.

"How you doin'?" I said.

"How YOU doin'?"

"How YOU doin'?"

We usually do this for at least half an hour. I don't know why we think it's so funny. But it really cracks us up.

"How you doin'?"

"How YOU doin'?"

Saturday morning is when we go to the Student Center to study. Mainly we study air hockey, pinball, and the new PlayStation games. We don't like to mess up our weekends doing homework.

I checked out my three friends. Feenman and Crench are tall and thin and kinda dance when they walk—real loose. Belzer is short and pudgy. He looks like his name—he's definitely a *Belzer*.

I shook my head. "Yo—you dudes are looking shabby," I said. "What's up with your clothes? They're totally wrinkled—and they don't even fit!"

Feenman sighed. "Bernie, our room is too small," he said. "All three of us are jammed in so tight, we have to take turns breathing!"

"It used to be a broom closet," Belzer said.

"So? What's that got to do with your clothes?" I asked.

"There's no room for a closet. We keep all our stuff in a big pile on the floor," Crench said. "We can't tell whose is whose!"

"Look—I'm wearing Feenman's shirt," Belzer said. The shirt came down to his knees. He raised his arms. "See these armpit stains, Bernie? They're not mine—they're Feenman's!"

"It's so crowded," Feenman said, "we have to sleep standing up!"

"Dudes, I hope you're not complaining," I said. "I

hope you're not hinting that I should share *my* room."

Feenman squinted at me. "Well, Big B, you ARE all alone in that huge room...."

"You *know* I need a lot of space," I said. "I need space for plotting and planning and scheming." I put a hand on Feenman's shoulder. "And who do I plot and plan and scheme for? I do it all for *you* guys, right?"

"Right," Belzer agreed. "Who convinced Nurse Hanley that Skittles are actually vitamin pills? Bernie did."

"That was a good thing," Feenman and Crench muttered.

"And who got Mrs. Heinie to give us extra credit if we don't burp up our breakfast in class?" Belzer asked. "Bernie did."

"That was a good thing, too," Feenman and Crench said.

"I'm always thinking of you guys," I said. "That's why I need the extra space."

And that's what this story is about—my extra space. Because guess what? An hour or two later I walked back to our dorm—Rotten House. I climbed the stairs to my room on the third floor.

And, yo! I stopped in the doorway—and stared at another boy unpacking a suitcase.

He had wavy, blond hair that glowed in the sunlight pouring through my window. He had a round face with big, blue eyes and rosy cheeks. He turned to me and flashed me a warm smile, his blue eyes twinkling.

"Who—who ARE you?" I stammered.

"I'm Angel Goodeboy," he said.

"No. Really," I said. "Who are you, and what are you doing in my room?"

Chapter 2

A BAD ALLERGY

The boy pulled a sweater from his suitcase and carefully folded it. He flashed me another smile. "I'm Angel Goodeboy," he said again. He walked over and shook my hand.

What was *up* with this guy? I stared at him. I'd never met a kid who shook hands before!

"Well, I'm sorry, dude," I said. "But you're in the wrong room. I'm Bernie Bridges. This is my room."

His cheeks turned bright red. He really *did* look like an angel. He just needed a halo, and he'd be perfect.

"I'm in the wrong room?" he gasped. "Oh, my gosh and goodness! I'm so sorry. Mrs. Heinie showed me in here."

"I guess Mrs. Heinie didn't clean her glasses this morning," I said.

Mrs. Heinie is our fourth-grade teacher and dorm mother. She is so nearsighted, she can't find her nose without a map!

"She made a mistake," I said. "Let me help you get packed up again."

"Oh, my gosh and goodness! I'm so, so, so sorry," he said. "I hope you will forgive me."

"No problem," I said. "Just pack up your stuff. Maybe you could share the room across the hall with Feenman, Crench, and Belzer. There's plenty of room over there."

I heard footsteps in the hall, then a voice in the doorway. "Oh. Have you two boys met?" I turned to see Mrs. Heinie peering at us through her thick glasses.

I flashed her my best smile. "Mrs. Heinie, you're looking wonderful!" I said. "That red bracelet on your arm—is it new? Very pretty!"

"I'm not wearing a red bracelet," she said. "I have a skin rash."

"Well, it looks very nice on you," I said. "I'm just helping the new kid pack up. He's in the wrong room."

Angel clasped his chubby little hands together. "I'm so, so, so, so sorry," he said. "I don't want to crowd Bernie's space."

Mrs. Heinie made a choking sound. "He's in the right room, Bernie. You'll just have to learn to *share*."

"But—but—but—" I sputtered.

I pulled Mrs. H. into the hall. "You *know* I can't have a roommate," I whispered to her. "I brought a doctor's note. I'm allergic."

I sneezed as hard as I could.

Mrs. Heinie wiped off the front of her sweater.

"See?" I said. "That Angel kid is making me sneeze already!"

I grabbed my neck. "My throat—it's closing up," I whispered. "Hard to breathe. I'm allergic to roommates. You understand, right?"

Mrs. Heinie stepped back into the room. Angel

was waiting patiently, hands in his khaki pockets.

"Angel is staying," Mrs. H. said. "I put him in here, Bernie, because I hope a little bit of his *goodness* will rub off on you!"

Angel's eyes twinkled again. I'm not sure how he made them twinkle like that. He flashed us another angelic smile.

"Mrs. H., please—" I begged. "I'm allergic to that smile! Look. It's making me ITCH all over!" I started scratching my whole body.

Mrs. Heinie scowled at me. "I don't want any trouble from you," she growled. "And don't try to teach him any of your sneaky tricks. He's a *good* boy, and he'd better stay that way!"

Angel's little red mouth formed a pout. "Oh, my gosh and goodness. I'm sorry if you don't want me, Bernie," he said in a soft, sad voice. "I'll stay out of your way. I'll stay in that corner over there." He pointed.

"Tell you what," he said. "I'll sleep in the closet. And in the morning I'll get dressed out in the hall. You won't even see me."

Mrs. Heinie squinted at me. "Do you see what an

angel he is? See how kind and generous?"

I started scratching my chest and arms. "Mrs. H., check it out. He's making me ITCH again! Please— he has to go!"

I had to do something. *No way* I could share my room with an *angel*!

But what could I do?

Chapter 3

HE ACTS LIKE AN ANGEL

I scratched so hard, I shredded my T-shirt. But Mrs. Heinie paid no attention.

She pointed. "Angel, why don't you take that bed by the night table?"

"But that's MY bed!" I cried.

Angel shook his head. "I don't want to be a bother," he said. "I don't want to take Bernie's bed away from him." He grinned at me. "I'll sleep UNDER the bed. Bernie won't even know I'm here."

He dropped onto his hands and knees and looked under my bed. "It's a tight fit," he said. "But I don't mind. If it will make Bernie happy."

"Angel, you're so GOOD!" Mrs. Heinie gushed. Behind her thick glasses she had tears in her eyes. "Angel will take the bed. No more talk."

Angel's grin grew wider.

Everyone knows I'm a talker, not a fighter. So why did I have the sudden urge to punch the kid in the stomach?

Maybe because I knew what he was doing. He was trying to out-scheme me, the king of schemes. That angel act *had to be an act.*

The dude was too good to be true! I knew I had to keep my guard up. What was he *really* up to?

Mrs. Heinie turned to me. "I'll get you a cot, Bernie. I'm sure you'll get used to it."

"A c-c-cot?" I stammered. "But I'm allergic—"

She pressed a hand over my mouth to shut me up. "And now that you're sharing your room," she said, "take down that *awful* poster on the wall."

I spun around. Could she be talking about my *favorite* poster? The big color poster of ME?

"I can't take it down," I told her. "Every time I look at it, it *inspires* me. It reminds me to be GREAT!"

Angel dug around in his suitcase. "I brought a poster that might inspire us BOTH!" he said. He pulled out a poster and unrolled it. Then he held it up for us to see.

A poster of naked angels with white, fluffy wings and baby faces, floating in the clouds.

I wanted to hurl. Naked angels hanging on *my* wall?!

Mrs. Heinie clapped her hands together. "How *beautiful!*" she cried. "Here, Angel, I'll help you put that up."

They pulled down the awesome Bernie Bridges poster and carried it to the closet. Then they hung the naked, baby-faced angel poster in its place.

My head swam. The room spun in front of me.

This CAN'T be happening to me! What am I going to DO?

Chapter 4

BEST FRIENDS

Mrs. Heinie patted Angel on the shoulder. She stepped back to admire the poster. I could see that Angel had her wrapped around his little finger.

What was his angle? I knew he was up to *something*.

Before I could duck away, Angel put an arm around my shoulders. "Bernie is such a cool guy," he said to Mrs. H. "I think we're going to be *best* friends—forever."

Yuck.

"Bernie could *use* a friend like you," Mrs. Heinie replied.

"About that cot—" I said.

"Mrs. Heinie, I *love* that awesome sweater you're wearing," Angel said. "What color is that? Lime green?"

Actually, it was *puke* green. But Mrs. Heinie was eating up Angel's compliment. The kid was stealing my act!

"I was just going to say that," I told Mrs. H. "That shade of green goes so well with your...uh...skin."

"Bernie, I'm counting on you to help Angel move in," she said. She smiled at Angel. "Let me know if there's anything I can do for you, Sweet-ums."

Sweet-ums?

You've gotta be *joking*!

She turned and walked off down the hall.

Angel picked up a stack of neatly folded T-shirts. "Is there a dresser drawer I could use?" he asked. "Or is it all full with your stuff?"

"Well..." I started.

"If it's full," he said, "I can keep all my clothes in a cardboard box."

Dudes, do you *believe* this kid?!

"I think I can spare half a drawer," I said. "Half the *bottom* drawer."

"Oh, thank you! Thank you!" he cried. "Everyone told me you're an awesome dude!"

"Well, yeah. That's true," I said. "Well…go ahead. Take a *whole* drawer."

What did I care? He wouldn't be here for long.

Once I got the Bernie B. brain into motion, I knew I could get Angel flying out of here. No problem.

I looked across the hall. Feenman, Crench, and Belzer weren't in their room.

When I turned back, I saw that Angel had tacked up another poster. A poster of Angel—wearing wings and a halo over his head.

Oh, puke!

I pinched myself really hard. I *had* to be dreaming this!

He grinned at me. "I see you're admiring my poster. I'm so, so, so glad you like it."

I shut my eyes, trying to
make him—*and* the poster—
disappear. No luck. When I
opened them, he was sitting at
my computer, typing hard.

I hurried over. "What are
you doing?" I asked.

"I'm e-mailing my

brother, Evan Lee," he said. He typed some more. "I'm telling him what an awesome roommate I have."

I rolled my eyes. "Evan Lee Goodeboy? Are you *kidding* me?"

"Then I'm gonna e-mail my other brother," Angel said. "His name is *also* Angel Goodeboy."

I stared at him. He has the same name as *you?*"

Angel nodded. "Yeah. We're twins. Twin angels. Ha-ha."

Was he putting me on?

"And your parents couldn't think of *another* name for him?" I asked.

"I guess they just like Angel," he said. He typed for a while.

I started to leave the room—and then stopped. "Whoa! Wait a minute!" I cried. "My History report. I left it on the computer."

He scrunched up his face. "Oh, my gosh and goodness!" he said in a whisper. "Was that your work? I think I accidentally *deleted* it."

Chapter 5

BANG THAT HEAD!

I started to choke. I grabbed my throat. "D-d-deleted?" I gasped. "I...I worked *three weeks* on that report!"

Angel jumped up. "I'm SOOOOOO sorry!" he said. "I can't believe I did that. I was bad. BAD!"

I squinted at him. Was he for REAL?

"So sorry! So sorry! So sorry!" he cried, hopping up and down. "My bad! My bad! I have to punish myself!"

He started banging his forehead against the wall. THUD, THUD, THUD-THUD.

I leaped across the room. I grabbed him by the shoulders and tried to pull him away from the wall. As I was tugging, Feenman and Crench burst into the room.

"What's up, Bernie?" Feenman asked. "Why are you banging that kid's head against the wall?"

"Me? Banging?" I said. "No way! You see—"

"What are you doing to the poor guy?" Crench asked.

Angel had tears running down his cheeks. His forehead was bright red from all the banging. "It's okay," he sobbed. "He didn't mean it. Really. He didn't mean to hurt me. He was just kidding around."

Feenman and Crench led Angel over to the bed. "You've got a pretty good bump on your head," Feenman said.

Crench turned to me. "Bernie, who *is* this kid? Why were you giving his head a workout?"

"I didn't *touch* him!" I said.

"That's right," Angel said. "It was all my fault. Don't blame him. He just didn't want to share his computer."

Feenman and Crench glared at me.

"I'm new here," Angel said. "At my old school we all shared."

"You can use my laptop," Crench said. "The *b* and *d* keys are broken. But who uses *b* and *d* that much?"

"Thanks," Angel said. "My name is Angel Goodeboy. Bernie and I are new best friends. And I know you guys will be good friends, too."

I couldn't stand it. Couldn't Feenman and Crench see what a phony this kid was? He was acting all innocent. But he was evil. I *knew* he was evil.

I had to get out of there. I watched Feenman and Crench trying to cheer up Angel, and it made my stomach heave.

I hurried outside to get some fresh air.

And as I passed the girls' dorm, I saw April-May June. Her blond ponytail waved in the wind. Her blue eyes sparkled like jewels. Dudes, are you beginning to see how I feel about April-May?

She's the hottest girl in school. And she feels the same way about me. She just doesn't know it yet.

"April-May—wait up!" I shouted. "Hey—wait up!"

Chapter 6

HE SNIFFS HIS ARMPITS

April-May whipped around so hard, her ponytail smacked her in the face. "I *can't* wait up, Bernie," she said. "I'm in a big hurry."

"A big hurry?" I said. "To do what?"

"To get away from you," she said.

"Ha-ha-ha." I laughed. She has an *awesome* sense of humor. I knew she was kidding. "Where are you going?" I asked.

She flipped her ponytail behind her. "To the library. You know. The place where they have books."

"I *love* books," I said. My heart started to pound.

"Books are my favorite thing for reading. Maybe you and I could read one together."

"Good idea," she said. "Maybe when I pull out all my hair and tattoo your name on my head."

"Could that be on Friday?" I asked.

She started to walk away. I hurried after her. "Friday night is movie night at the Student Center," I said. "Would you like to go with me?"

She spun around again. "Bernie, who is that new boy in your dorm? I hear he's really cute."

I gulped. "Angel? Cute? You wouldn't like him. He has hair growing out of his nose, and he licks it."

She stomped down hard on my foot.

"OWWWW!" I let out a scream and stumbled back. "Why did you do that?"

"Just felt like it," she said. "Now tell me about this new kid."

"What about my question about Friday night?" I said.

"I already forgot it," April-May said.

Flora and Fauna—the Peevish twins—came running up. The twins are identical. They are both short and thin and have brown hair and brown eyes.

There's only one way to tell which is which: Fauna is the one on the left.

"We heard there's a cute new guy in your dorm," Fauna said.

"I heard it first," Flora said.

"Did not," Fauna said. "I heard it *before* he even came here."

"I heard it before that!" her sister said.

They started slapping each other and tearing at each other's hair. April-May and I had to pull them apart.

"So? What's he like?" Flora asked.

"You wouldn't like him," I said. "He's very hairy, and he grunts. He doesn't talk. He scratches his

armpits, and he sniffs them. And he smells like two-day-old diarrhea."

Good description, huh?

All three girls stared at me.

"You're lying," April-May said.

"Yeah. He's lying," Fauna agreed.

"Maybe a little," I replied.

"We're having a party at the girls' dorm Tuesday afternoon," April-May said. "Could you send the new kid over?"

"He's not ready for a party," I said. "Too shy. I'm trying to show him the ropes. Break him in slowly. Maybe I could come in his place."

"I don't think so," April-May said.

"We heard he's a total angel," Flora said. "Send him over, Bernie."

"I get to meet him first," Fauna said.

"No. Me," her sister shot back. "Because I heard about him first."

"I heard about him last year," Fauna said.

"I heard about him two years ago," Flora replied.

SLAP! SLAP! SLAP!

They started pounding each other again. It was pretty ugly.

April-May jogged off to the library. I turned and slumped back to the dorm, thinking hard.

Maybe I should give Angel a break. Maybe I was wrong about him. Maybe he *did* want to be best friends. Maybe he *wasn't* evil.

I climbed the stairs to my room. I'll try being nice, I decided.

After all, who on this planet is nicer than Bernie B.?

I stepped into the room with a dazzling smile on my face. Glanced around—and let out a

GAAAAAACK!

Chapter 7

GAAAAACK!

My mouth dropped open. My tongue hung out. I made HUNH-HUNH panting sounds. And I stared at the posters tacked on the walls. More angel posters. Dozens of them.

Little baby angels with pink cheeks and fluffy wings. All with Angel's face. Flying all over MY walls!

"I hope you don't mind," Angel said. He was sitting on MY bed. "The angels are just so CUTE!" He giggled. "And Mrs. Heinie really liked them, too. She helped me tack them up."

GAAAAAAACK!

"Hunh-hunh-hunh," I said.

"Oh, my gosh and goodness. I've been really busy," Angel said. He jumped up and moved to the dresser. "I put my clothes in the bottom drawer like you said, Bernie. But I looked in the other drawers. And I saw your stuff was all wrinkled and jammed in."

"So?" I asked.

"So I pulled everything out," Angel said. "I piled your stuff on the closet floor, where you'll have more room."

My mouth dropped open even lower. My jaw was hanging around my knees! "You—you took over the whole dresser? You threw all my clothes on the closet floor?" I stammered.

"Don't thank me," Angel said. He flashed me one of his sparkling smiles. "I'm happy to help you out, Bernie, since you're my new best friend."

GAAAAACK!

I knew it. I KNEW it. It didn't take me long to figure out this dude's plan. Forget the angel act. He wanted to take over my room. He wanted to force me OUT!

"I totally like those two tall, thin friends of yours," he said. "Feenman and Crench? They were so nice to me. I had to reward them."

"Reward them?" I said weakly.

He nodded. "Yeah. I gave them a bunch of candy bars I found in your closet. It made them really happy."

I let out a shriek. "My Nutty Nutty Bars? You *gave* them my Nutty Nutty Bars? But I get *two dollars each* for those candy bars!"

Angel's angelic smile spread until I thought his cheeks would burst. "It's nice to do *good* things for others. Don't you agree?"

GAAAAAACK!

If he wanted to do good things, why did he have to use MY candy bars?

I lurched across the hall into Feenman and Crench's room. They were both stretched out on their bunk beds, stuffing their faces with chocolate bars.

"Get up. We've got work to do," I said. "We've gotta get that new kid out of my room. Out of Rotten House! He doesn't belong in our dorm."

CHOMP, CHOMP, CHOMP!

They didn't answer me for a long time. Their cheeks were bulging with Nutty Nutty Bars.

"Big B, Angel is a great guy," Feenman said finally. He had chocolate smeared on his cheeks and chin. And how did he get it on his forehead? "He gave us all these Nutty Nutty Bars—for *free*!"

"Yeah. Free," Crench muttered, chewing hard. He was chewing up the wrappers and swallowing them.

"But they were MINE!" I cried. "Don't you see? He's a THIEF!"

CHOMP, CHOMP, CHOMP!

"That's harsh, Bernie," Feenman said. "Give the kid a break."

"Yeah," Crench agreed. "He's a good dude. Very generous."

"But—but—" I sputtered.

"You're just jealous," Feenman said. "Because he's so good looking."

"Huh? Good-looking?" I cried. "Does he have dimples like these?" I flashed my prize-winning dimples.

CHOMP, CHOMP, CHOMP!

They didn't answer me.

"Dudes, he put up pictures of angels all over my room," I said. "How can I sleep with angel eyes staring at me from everywhere?"

"I think they're kinda cute," Crench said.

GAAAAACK!

"Angel said he could get us free Foamy Root Beer," Feenman said. "And free doughnuts."

"And he said he'd try to get us a bigger room," Crench added.

Wow. Angel was turning my own friends against me. I had to do something—fast.

But *fast* wouldn't be fast enough—because Angel had *more* plans to take over the dorm and push me out.

And they started the very next morning with a really big shock!

Chapter 8

ANGEL IS A GOOD BIRD

I woke up with sunshine beaming into my eyes. "Huh? Where am I?" I lifted my head and squinted into the light. Oh, yeah."

It took me a few seconds to remember that I was now sleeping in a cot under the window in my room. With a sigh I raised myself higher and glanced over at MY bed.

Angel sat on the side of the bed in his striped pajamas. And what was that fat

lump next to him?

Gassy! My pet! My bulldog! Snoring away at the foot of the bed.

"Hey—what's up with him?" I cried. "That's *my* dog!"

Angel flashed me the first smile of the morning. Sunshine shimmered around him, a halo of light above his golden hair.

"Gassy seems to like dog biscuits," he said.

I shook myself awake. "Huh? Dog biscuits?"

Angel nodded. "I gave him a *whole box* for his breakfast."

"But—but—" I stammered. "That will make him *sick*."

The fat bulldog let out a snort. He had a big smile on his face.

Angel raised his hands to his cheeks. "Oh, my gosh and goodness. I hope I didn't do anything wrong," he said. "I'd never do *anything* to hurt you or your doggie, Bernie pal."

He petted Gassy's big lump of a head. The dog sighed softly. "Look—he likes me," Angel said. "I think he's MY dog now!"

My bed. My dresser. My friends. My DOG?

"No way!" I cried.

I jumped off the cot. "Come with me, boy," I said to Gassy. "You know who you belong to. Come over here with me."

I grabbed the big dog's collar and started to tug him off Angel's bed.

Grrrrrrrr. Gassy bared his teeth and snarled at me.

"Whoa!" I jumped back.

Angel laughed. Gassy raised his head, stuck out his fat tongue, and started to lick Angel's face. That made Angel laugh even harder.

"Sorry, Bernie. What can I say? He loves ME now!"

I turned away and walked over to the birdcage in one corner. Maybe a box of lousy dog biscuits made Gassy a traitor. But I still had my sweet parrot.

I pulled the cover off the cage and leaned down to greet the beautiful bird. "Good morning, Lippy," I said. "How are you today, sweetie?"

Lippy tilted his green head. He gazed out at me with one eye.

"*Angel is a good bird!*" he squawked. "*Angel is a good bird! Bernie bites! Bernie bites big time!*"

GAAAAAACK!

I reached in to pet my adorable parrot. *PLOP.* He dropped something hot and sticky into my hand.

GAAAAACK AGAIN!

Angel had turned *both* of my pets against me.

What next?

Chapter 9

BREAKFAST IN BED

I dropped back onto the cot to think.
I knew I could *think* my way out of this.
No one thinks like Bernie B. when I put
my mind to it.

BRRRAAAAAP.

"Eeew! Phewww!" Angel moaned.
He pinched his nose shut. He started fan-
ing the air. "Why does my new dog smell
so bad?"

"Maybe it's because of the entire

box of dog biscuits you fed him," I muttered.

I heard heavy footsteps in the hall. Belzer stepped in, carrying a big breakfast tray. The Dining Hall is just *too noisy* in the morning. So Belzer brings me breakfast in bed.

Good kid, Belzer.

"Good morning, Belzer," I said, climbing under the covers. "Whoa. Wait. What's that T-shirt you're wearing?"

Belzer stuck out his chest so I could read the front. In big red letters, it read: DON'T LOOK AT ME.

"Great," I said. "That shirt is gonna win you a lot of friends."

He squinted at me. "You think so?"

Belzer buys all his T-shirts at a store called Crumby Shirts No One Else Will Wear.

"Never mind," I said. "What do you have for breakfast this morning?"

Belzer gazed down at the tray. "Scrambled eggs with bacon and sausage, blueberry pancakes, cornflakes, and two chocolate-chip muffins," he said.

My mouth watered. "Excellent," I said. "A *small* breakfast. I don't like to overdo it in the morning. Just set it down in my lap. Gently. My knees bruise easily."

Belzer blinked a few times. "But it isn't for *you*, Bernie," he said.

I laughed. "Belzer, what did I tell you about making jokes? Remember, I said you weren't quite *ready* for jokes yet?"

Belzer blinked a few more times. "I wasn't joking, Big B. This breakfast is for Angel."

"Huh?" My brain started to spin. "Breakfast in bed for Angel?"

"It was my idea, Bernie," Angel said. "You've been looking really pale. You need fresh air, pal. A nice walk to the

Dining Hall every morning will be good for you."

Belzer set the tray down on Angel's lap.

Angel picked up a chocolate-chip muffin and started to chew off the top. "I'm only thinking of you, roomie," he said to me. "You're my best friend, and I want you to be healthy."

He turned to Belzer. "Would you slice the sausage for me? I like to have it in small chunks before I start to eat."

"No problem," Belzer said. "I got you the soft bacon you asked for. I tasted each piece to make sure it was soft, Angel."

GAAAAAACK!

I couldn't take it anymore. I *never* totally lose it—but I TOTALLY LOST IT.

I leaped out of bed. I grabbed the edge

of the tray. I let out an angry roar and started to tug the tray off Angel's lap.

"Bernie?"

I heard a voice behind me.

"Bernie? What's going *on* in here?"

I let go of the tray and spun around. "Good morning, Mrs. Heinie," I said.

"You're looking beautiful today. I love what you've done with your single eyebrow."

"Never mind my eyebrow," she snapped. She squinted at me through her thick glasses. "What were you fighting about?"

"Me? Fighting?" I said. "Oh, no. You've got it wrong, Mrs. H. Belzer and I—we were treating my new roommate. A special welcome. We were giving him breakfast in bed."

Angel rested the tray on Gassy. Then he climbed out of bed. "I know Bernie was trying to be nice," he told Mrs. Heinie.

"But I don't really *like* breakfast in bed. I'd much rather be in the Dining Hall with all my new friends."

Mrs. Heinie beamed at Angel. "You're such a good boy," she gushed.

Then she turned to me, and her smile became a scowl. "Bernie, stop trying to teach Angel bad habits!"

I took a slice of bacon from the tray and slid it into my mouth. "Bad habits? Huh? Me?"

Chapter 10

THE GREAT MAN?

The next morning was a hot, steamy Monday. I woke up slowly, feeling sweaty, my pajamas stuck to my skin.

I opened my eyes—and saw Angel, already dressed. He smiled at me. I had to shut my eyes. The glow from his teeth was *painful*!

His yellow, green, and purple school tie was perfectly tied. The brass buttons on his school blazer gleamed as if he'd polished them.

I yawned. "Where's Belzer? Isn't he bringing breakfast?"

Angel tugged me up. "Oh, my gosh and goodness. Bernie, hurry. It's my first day of class. I can't wait!"

Oh, wow. Was he for real?

"Please walk me to the School House," he said. "I'm not sure where to find it."

I yawned again. "Just walk in any direction," I said. "You'll get there sooner or later."

But he dragged me out of bed and shoved my uniform at me. A few minutes later I was leading him across the Great Lawn toward the School House building where all our classes are held.

Kids poured out of the three dorms, laughing and talking. I waved to April-May June, but she didn't wave back.

I saw my buddies Feenman and Crench tossing a Frisbee back and forth. Those crazy dudes probably forgot it was Monday.

I pointed to the tall, stone building at the far end of the Great Lawn. "That's the School House," I said. "We call it Mouse House. Know why? Because it's *infested*! Hope you don't mind a mouse or two climbing up your legs."

Angel laughed. He thought I was kidding.

I heard a thud of footsteps, turned, and saw my friend Beast stampeding toward us. Beast is a weird guy. He's a little too hairy to be human. But no one knows *what* he is.

Sometimes he chases after squirrels on all fours. And when he catches one, it isn't pretty.

"Yo, Beast!" I called.

But he ran up to Angel and started licking Angel's hand. "You and me. Good buddies," he grunted. Then he scampered off, chasing after a blowing leaf.

I turned to Angel. "Beast is *your* friend now? How did *that* happen?"

Angel shrugged. "I gave him a box of dog biscuits, too."

I clenched my fists. This guy was stealing all my friends.

The sun beamed down on us. Sweat poured down my forehead. I loosened my tie a little.

"Hey, there goes the Great Man—Headmaster Upchuck," Angel said. He pointed.

The GREAT MAN?

I turned and saw the Headmaster doing his morning run across the grass. Mr. Upchuck is as short as a third grader, bald, and red-faced. He waddles like a duck when he runs.

"Wow," Angel said, "the Great Man looks hot and tired." Angel picked up a fallen tree limb from the grass. "Maybe I can help Mr. Upchuck out."

"What are you going to do with that?" I asked.

"This will make a good walking stick," Angel replied. He started to run, holding the tree limb in front of him.

I should have warned Angel that the Headmaster

doesn't like kids to talk to him. Kids make him nervous. But I didn't say a word. I just stood and watched.

Upchuck was jogging slowly toward Pooper's Pond.

Angel waved the stick as he ran. "Sir!" he shouted. "I've got something for you!"

Startled, Upchuck lurched to a stop.

Angel couldn't stop himself. He ran right into him.

The tree limb rammed Upchuck in the back.

And the Headmaster went flying into the pond!

For a little guy, he made a very big splash.

I watched as he started thrashing and kicking and splashing. "HELP ME!" the Great Man screamed. "I can't SWIM! HELLLP!"

The pond is only four feet deep. But it was over Upchuck's head.

Time for me to be the big hero.

I pulled the long stick from Angel and went running to the edge of the pond. I waved it over him. "Grab on, sir!" I called. "I'll fish you out. Grab on!"

He splashed and thrashed some more. Then his little hands grabbed the limb.

"I've got you, sir," I said. I tugged with all my strength, and he came sliding onto the muddy shore. "Bernie B. to the rescue!"

"Why—why—why—" he sputtered. He shook his whole body—like a wet dog. Water went flying off him.

"Bernie," he snarled, squeezing the soaked knees of his pants. "Get to my office. Now. You knocked me into the water. One of your funny jokes? Well, soon you're not going to be laughing!"

"No! Not true!" I cried. "It wasn't *me*, sir. It's not my stick. It—it was the new kid. The new kid—"

I spun around. Where WAS he?

Angel?

Angel had vanished.

"It was the new kid," I said. "You've gotta believe me, sir. It was Angel Goodeboy. He—"

"IN MY OFFICE! NOW!" the Great Man shouted.

As I slunk away, somewhere in the bushes behind me I heard a soft giggle.

Angel's giggle.

Chapter 11

A SECRET ADMIRER

That afternoon I went to see my buddies Feenman and Crench in their room. They were down on the floor. I saw an open can of Pringles potato chips next to their bunk beds. They had the chips spread out all over the floor.

"Dudes, what's up?" I asked.

Feenman didn't look up. He had his head close to the floor and was studying the chips.

"We're trying to find one that's different," Crench said.

Feenman sighed. "So far, they're all the same."

"Why are you looking for one that's different?" I asked.

Feenman shrugged. "I don't know."

Crench shrugged, too. "Something to do, I guess."

"Mr. Boring said we should do experiments," Feenman said. (Mr. Boring is our Science teacher.) "I like doing experiments with chips because then I can eat them." He grabbed up a handful of chips and shoved them into his mouth.

"How do they taste?" Crench asked.

"Mmmph-mmmph. All the same," Feenman said.

"Interesting," Crench said. "Very interesting. We should experiment with the nacho cheese flavor, too. And maybe garlic and onion."

I let out an angry cry and kicked the Pringles can across the room.

"Big B, what's your problem?" Feenman asked.

"Didn't you hear?" I said. "I'm on probation."

They both gasped. Chewed-up chips dribbled out of Feenman's mouth. He picked the sticky blob up from the floor and shoved it back into his mouth. "Probation? Is that good or bad?"

"Bad," I said. "Very bad."

"What does it mean?" Crench asked.

I shook my head. "It means that Angel Goodeboy is trying to get me kicked out of school. First he wanted my room all to himself. Now he wants me totally gone."

Feenman climbed to his feet. "But Angel is a good guy, Bernie," he said. "Look. He gave us these chips."

"Yeah. You've gotta give the dude a chance," Crench said.

I gritted my teeth. "See?" I cried. "He's even got YOU guys fooled! He's not an angel. He's EVIL!" I started pacing back and forth and accidentally stepped on the chips.

CRUNCH, CRUNCH, CRUNCH.

"Watch out," Feenman said. "I gotta *eat* those!"

"Don't you guys see what he's doing?" I shouted. "He's got all my friends fooled. And Mrs. Heinie, too. What am I gonna do?"

Angel appeared in the doorway. He grinned at us. "Dudes, I hope you weren't talking about me!" He laughed. "Sorry you got into trouble this morning, Bernie."

Before I could answer, Belzer pushed his way into the room. He was carrying a big bouquet of flowers wrapped in a paper cone.

"Are those for me?" Angel cried. He made a grab for them. "Probably from my mother back home. Or maybe my big sister, Honey Goodeboy. Or maybe my other sister, Angelcake Goodeboy."

Belzer pulled them away from him. "They're not for you," he said. "They're for Bernie."

I took the flowers and sniffed them. "Well, of course, they're for me," I told Angel. "From one of my many admirers."

I carried them into my room. The guys followed me. "I know who they're from!" I said. "April-May has finally come to her senses. She's *crazy* about me! Look at these flowers. Awesome! I knew she'd finally wake up."

I found a small card inside the paper cone. I pulled it out. My fingers trembled as I started to open it....

Were they really from April-May?

Chapter 12

TRAITORS

No. They were not.

I took Feenman and Crench aside. "I forgot," I said. "I ordered these flowers. From that store we passed in town—Flowers 'n' Junk."

They squinted at me. "You ordered flowers to give to *yourself?*" Crench asked.

"No." I whispered because I didn't want Angel to hear. "They're for Mrs. Heinie. I'm gonna give them to her after dinner tonight."

"Huh?" Feenman said. "Why?"

"I've got to win her back to my side," I said.

"Maybe she'll believe me when I tell her that Angel is really a *devil.*"

"But he's *not* a devil," Crench said. "He gave us free candy bars."

"He's a good dude," Feenman said. "Check out how he's feeding the dog."

"But it's MY dog!" I cried. "And MY candy bars."

"ANGEL IS A GOOD BIRD!" Lippy squawked.

"ANGEL IS A GOOD BIRD!"

"Has *everyone* turned traitor?" I cried.

Feenman and Crench headed back to their room. Angel and I were alone. I set the flowers down on my cot. Angel was feeding Gassy dog biscuit after dog biscuit.

BRRRAAAAAP.

"Eew! He stinks! He stinks!" Angel gasped, holding his nose.

"That's why we didn't name him *Flowers*," I said. It was a joke, but Angel didn't laugh.

He tossed the empty dog biscuit box to the floor. "Bernie, who is this April-May June you were talking about?"

"She's my girlfriend," I said. "Are you going to give her a box of dog biscuits, too?" Another joke. Angel didn't seem to *get* jokes.

He stared at me. "Your girlfriend?"

"Only she doesn't know it yet," I said.

He nodded. I could see his little brain spinning. "Maybe I can help you," he said.

Uh-oh.

"Help me?" I replied.

"I owe you a favor," Angel said, "since I ACCIDENTALLY got you into trouble with Headmaster Upchuck this morning."

"Yeah. Accidentally," I muttered.

"Girls all like me," Angel said. "They think I'm cute and cuddly. Maybe I can get April-May to go to the movies with you."

I shook my head so hard, my ears rattled. "No way!" I shouted. "Don't even *think* about it!"

I took a few angry steps toward him. "I'm warning you—stay away from April-May."

He pretended he didn't hear me. "I'll give it a try," he said. "That's what *best friends* are for—right, good buddy?"

Chapter 13

GOOD
BUDDY

The next afternoon was gray and cool. I felt a few raindrops on my head as I walked across campus.

Where was I walking? I didn't care. Sometimes taking a long walk helps me think. And I was thinking hard—about guess who?

Yes. My new best friend. Only, when it came to Angel, I spelled *friend P-E-S-T*.

A few minutes before, Angel had stopped me in front of Rotten House. "Hey, good buddy. I talked to your girlfriend," he said.

Huh? I felt a heavy rock form in my stomach.

Angel patted me on the shoulder. "She said she'll go to the movies with you. No problem."

I opened my mouth in shock. He didn't let me say anything. He clapped a hand over my mouth.

"Don't thank me," he said. "You're my good buddy. You know I'm always happy to do you a favor. Gosh and golly. You're my best friend. Please—don't thank me."

I didn't thank him. I didn't know what to say.

Did he really talk to April-May? Did she really say she'd go with me to Movie Night?

I continued my walk, thinking about it. I barely noticed the raindrops. I wasn't even watching where I was walking.

Suddenly—"OWWWWWWW!" I let out a scream. I hit the ground hard, tackled from behind.

A heavy weight fell on top of me, pinning me to the grass.

"Guess who?" a voice said.

I didn't have to guess. I knew it was Jennifer Ecch.

Jennifer Ecch, the biggest, strongest, toughest, tackling-est girl in school. I call her Nightmare Girl.

She jumped up. Then she pulled me to my feet and dusted me off. "Hi, Honey Face," she said.

"*Please* don't call me Honey Face," I begged.

She tenderly smoothed back my hair. With both hands! She smoothed so hard, hanks of my hair came out!

Do you know how *embarrassing* it is to be in fourth grade and have a girl totally in *love* with you?

"Jennifer, why are your hands so sticky?" I cried.

She grinned. "I was eating a candy apple, Sugar Nostrils."

"PLEASE don't call me Sugar Nostrils!"

She hugged me. I heard at least eight ribs snap. "Of COURSE I'll go to the movies with you!" Jennifer boomed. "You didn't have to send that new kid to ask me."

She hugged me tighter. I couldn't breathe. Didn't she see that my face had turned blue? "Sweety Neck, why didn't you ask me yourself?" she said.

My mouth dropped open. My eyes rolled around in my head. My ears rattled again. "Excuse me?"

"That cute new kid. Angel," Jennifer said. "He said you wanted to ask me to Movie Night. He said you were too shy to ask me yourself."

I clamped my eyes shut. *Angel got me again!*

Jennifer covered my arms with sticky, candy-apple kisses. Rain started to pour down on us. Jennifer didn't seem to care. She didn't stop till my arms were totally sticky and wet.

Finally I slithered out of her grasp and slunk away.

I had to find Angel.

I told you—I'm a talker, not a fighter. But I kept clenching and unclenching my fists as I trudged through the pounding rain.

I was soaked by the time I reached Rotten House. My shoes squished as I climbed the stairs to my room. Oops. I mean, OUR room.

Angel was hunched over my computer. Probably deleting more homework of mine.

I burst into the room, shaking off water. "YO!" I let out an angry shout.

He turned. His smile faded quickly. "Bernie? What's wrong?"

I took a deep breath. *Calm, Bernie. Gotta be calm.*

"Why did you invite Jennifer to the movies for me?" I asked, clenching my teeth.

He wrinkled up his face. "Who?"

"Jennifer Ecch."

He slapped himself on the forehead. "You mean that wasn't April-May? I got the wrong girl?"

I gritted my teeth harder. Steam poured out of my

72

ears. "Yesssssss," I hissed. "You got the wrong girl."

"Oh, my gosh and goodness! My bad!" Angel said. "I'm new here. I was only trying to help. I really thought she was April-May!"

I rolled my eyes. "Yeah. Sure."

"I WAS BAD! I WAS BAD!" Angel screamed. He stood up and started to bang his head against the wall.

THUD! THUD! THUD!

"I WAS BAD! I WAS BAD!"

I leaped across the room and grabbed him. I tried to pull him away from the wall.

And once again I heard Mrs. Heinie's startled cry from behind me. "Bernie! What are you doing to Angel?"

I spun around to face her. "Who? ME?" I cried.

"I've warned you about this," she said. "Come with me." She started to pull me from the room.

"Mrs. H.—wait!" I cried. I made a grab for the flowers. "I have something for you."

"I have something for *you*," she said. "Three hours of cleanup duty. Starting now."

"But—but—" I stuttered. "Mrs. Heinie, you know

I can't clean things. It makes my skin flake off. I have a doctor's note—"

"Three hours," she said, pulling me harder. "You can start by scrubbing the bathroom floors."

"*Scrub?* I don't know that word. Is that a foreign word?"

I tried to give her the flowers. But Angel swiped them from my hand.

Mrs. Heinie pulled me out into the hall. I turned

back. The last thing I saw was Angel, standing
there with a big grin on his face. He had
my flowers in one hand, and he was
happily waving good-bye to
me with the other.

Chapter 14

"ISN'T ANGEL AWESOME?"

Yes, it was the worst day of my life. I learned what *scrub* means. It's *not* on my list of 10,000 Favorite Words.

After three hours of scrubbing and rubbing and drubbing and grubbing and whatever else you do to make things sparkle and shine, I was toast. My hands swelled up to the size of baseball gloves. My heart thrummed. My knees wobbled. My tongue hung down to my shoes.

I staggered outside. The Great Lawn glistened with raindrops. The walk was dotted with puddles. I splashed right through them.

"Hey!" I cried out when I saw April-May June walking near the girls' dorm. I staggered after her.

She's so shy. She usually runs away when she sees me coming. But now she spun around with a big smile on her beautiful face.

"Isn't Angel *awesome?*" she gushed.

"Huh?" My eyes bulged.

"He asked me to Movie Night on Friday," April-May said. "And look—he gave me these flowers."

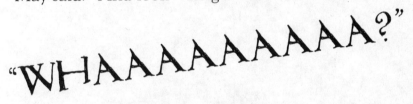

"WHAAAAAAAAA?"

I wailed. I stared at the bouquet in April-May's hand.

MY FLOWERS!

The flowers I bought to give Mrs. Heinie!

"Isn't Angel the sweetest?" April-May said, holding the flowers to her face and sniffing them.

"The sweetest," I muttered. My heart pounded. I felt weak. My knees folded. I sat down in a puddle.

Cold water seeped through my pants. I had a soaking wet butt. But who cares? I watched April-May run off, carrying my flowers.

Angel wants my room, my friends, my pets, and my *girlfriend*! I told myself.

I sat there for a few minutes, in a daze. Finally I pulled myself to my feet and started walking again.

Flora and Fauna, the Peevish twins, were standing by the statue of our school's founder, I. B. Rotten. They were slapping each other and pulling each other's hair and screaming a lot.

"What are you fighting about?" I asked.

"I saw Angel first!" Fauna screamed. "I get to hang out with him after class!"

"But he doesn't LIKE you!" Flora cried. "He likes me because I'm prettier!"

"Prettier?! Are you crazy?" her sister wailed. "We're IDENTICAL—remember?"

"I saw him first!"

"But I *talked* to him first!"

"OUCH!"

"OUCH!"

They slapped each other and tugged out hanks of each other's hair as they staggered away. Fighting over Angel...

"I can't take this anymore!" I cried. I sat down in another puddle and buried my head in my hands.

Across the grass I heard voices. I looked up and saw that spoiled rich kid, Sherman Oaks. My biggest enemy—from the other boys' dorm—the dorm we all hate—Nyce House.

Sherman was talking with Angel. He was show-ing off a new cell phone. I watched them from my seat in the puddle. They were watching a movie on Sherman's phone!

"Oh, wow." I buried my head in my hands again. Sherman *used* to brag about his expensive new toys to ME!

Angel was taking all my friends—and my *ene-mies*, too!

I had no choice. I had to prove to everyone what a bad-news dude Angel really was. If I didn't, I'd be sitting in rain puddles for the rest of the year.

Wait a minute!

Suddenly I had a plan.

Chapter 15

HOW TO TRAP AN ANGEL

First I had to get my best buddies, Feenman and Crench, back on my side. I had to show them the *truth* about Angel!

While Angel was out, hanging at the girls' dorm, I got a big bag of Nutty Nutty Candy Bars and carried it across the hall to their room. "Dudes, check it out!" I said.

I held open the bag. They each made a grab. I had to slap their hands away. "Look—don't touch!" I said.

"Bernie, aren't you going to *give* them to us?"

Crench asked. "Angel gave us Nutty Nutty Bars for free."

The word *free* made me choke. Feenman had to slap me on the back.

"*No way* I'm giving them to you," I said. "This is proof, dudes. Proof that Angel is a sneak and a thief."

"Bernie, give it a rest," Feenman said, shaking his head. "Everyone likes Angel."

"Are you going to let me prove it to you or not?" I asked.

They stared at the bag of candy. And they both started to drool. "What do we have to do?" Crench asked, wiping his chin with one hand.

"I'm gonna wait till Lights Out," I said. "Then I'll put this bag on my windowsill and pretend to go to sleep. You guys will hide in my closet. Then—"

"Huh? What did you just say?" Feenman asked. "Hide in your closet after Lights Out?"

"If Mrs. Heinie catches us—" Crench started.

"She won't catch you," I said. "You hide in the closet, and you watch. I'm betting that Angel steals the bag of candy off the windowsill and hides it somewhere."

"He isn't a thief," Crench said. "No way."

"You're wrong this time, Bernie," Feenman said. He made another grab for the candy bars. I had to slap his hand away again.

Every night before Lights Out Mrs. Heinie comes into each room. She shakes hands and says good night to every boy in the dorm. It's an old Rotten School tradition.

Tonight she shook Angel's hand and gave him a warm smile. "How are you boys getting along?" she asked him.

Angel returned her smile. "Like brothers," he said. "Bernie and I are best friends for life!"

Mrs. Heinie tucked him into his bed. Then she walked over to my cot and shook my hand. "Angel is a good boy," she said. "I hope you are learning from him, Bernie."

"We're all learning a *lot* from him, Mrs. H.," I said. "I wish there were *ten* more Angels in the dorm. Or maybe twenty. Then we could all be good all the time."

She rolled her eyes. "Give me a break," she muttered.

She started toward my buddies' room across the hall—and I realized I had to think fast. Feenman and Crench weren't in their room. They were hiding in my closet.

"Mrs. H., don't go in there," I called.

She squinted at me through her thick glasses. "Why not?"

"The smell," I said. "It's bad in there. Something died in that room about a week ago. And we can't find it. Feenman and Crench and Belzer are wearing gas masks. Don't go in. I know you have a very sensitive nose."

She frowned at me. "That's ridiculous." She started to open their door.

"They can't shake hands," I said. "They all have a bad skin rash. They've scratched all their skin off. Their hands are itching and oozing green and yellow stuff. Really, Mrs. H., you don't want to catch it."

She thought about that for a second. "Okay. Tell them I said good night." She clicked off the lights in my room.

I shut my eyes and listened to her footsteps as she climbed the stairs to her room in the attic. Bernie B.'s fast thinking saves the day again!

The closet door stood open an inch. I flashed Feenman and Crench a thumbs-up. "Good night, best friend," Angel said, yawning.

"Good night, Angel," I said. "Sweet dreams. And I mean *sweet*. Sweet as candy!" I glanced at the big bag of candy bars on the windowsill.

I knew Angel wouldn't be able to resist it. I knew he'd sneak out of bed in the darkness to steal my candy. And Feenman and Crench would see the truth about him.

I shut my eyes and pretended to go to sleep. I started to snore softly. I knew Angel wouldn't wait long.

Sure enough, a few minutes later he sat up. I watched him climb out of bed. I had my eyes closed to tiny slits. But I could see him perfectly. I watched him silently tiptoe across the room.

Yes. Yes! The little thief was falling for my trap!

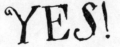

--- Chapter 16 ---

SCARED STIFF

I raised my head from the pillow. I knew Feenman and Crench were watching. I tensed my muscles and got ready to jump up. As soon as Angel grabbed the candy, I planned to race across the room and flash on the light.

I watched him tiptoe...tiptoe.

Hey. Wait. He didn't go to the windowsill. He tiptoed out of the room.

"Bernie, where's he going?" Crench called from the closet.

"Shh!" I warned. "Quiet. He'll be back in a few

88

seconds. And he'll grab the candy. Just watch."

"I'm getting a leg cramp in here," Feenman said.

"I'm getting a foot cramp!" Crench whispered.

"That's not *your* foot—that's mine!" Feenman said.

"Well, whose leg is this?" Crench said. "I can't tell in the dark."

"Quiet," I whispered. "Here he comes. He's back. Just keep your eyes on him."

Squinting, I saw Angel step into the doorway.

The light flashed on.

Uh-oh. He had Mrs. Heinie with him. "You just had a bad dream," she told Angel.

"It wasn't a dream," Angel said in a tiny voice. "I heard weird noises in the closet, Mrs. Heinie."

"Don't be afraid," Mrs. Heinie said.

I watched Angel cling to her arm. He was trembling. "There's a *monster* in there. I know there is! I heard it," he said. "I'm scared. Scared stiff! I'm *totally* scared!"

"There's nothing to be afraid of," Mrs. Heinie said. "Here. I'll show you."

She pulled open the closet door.

Feenman and Crench came stumbling out.

"Huh? What's going *on* here?" she cried. "What are you DOING in there?"

My two buddies stood there with their eyes bulging and their mouths hanging open. I knew I had to come to their rescue.

"Uh…I can explain," I said, jumping out of bed. I adjusted my pajama pants.

Think fast, Bernie. Think FAST.

"You see, Mrs. H., they get a little *cramped* with Belzer in that tiny room of theirs," I said. "So sometimes they like to stretch out in my closet."

"HUMPH!" Mrs. Heinie exclaimed. It was a powerful *HUMPH!* It almost blew me over.

"I should have known this was *your* idea, Bernie," she said. "Why were you trying to scare Angel like that?"

She didn't give me a chance to answer. She marched Feenman, Crench, and me downstairs. She gave us a half-hour lecture. "Why can't you all be as good as Angel Goodeboy?" she asked.

I gritted my teeth and slunk back up to my room. Angel was tucked into his bed, sound asleep. I glanced at the windowsill.

Of course. Big surprise. The bag of candy bars was
GONE.

Chapter 17

WILL THE PEA SOUP FLY?

"I know what Angel's next plan is," I said. "I know his next dirty trick."

We were hanging out at the statue of I. B. Rotten, our school's founder. I was sitting on Rotten's head. Feenman and Crench were filling in his eyes with black markers.

"Give it a rest, Bernie," Crench said. "You're just gonna get us into more trouble. Angel is a good guy. Everyone likes him."

"He's fooling everyone," I said. "Even you two guys."

Feenman painted big, black nostrils on the statue's nose. "I. B. Rotten is looking GOOD!" he said.

I. B.
ROTTEN

"Listen to me," I said. "I'm gonna prove what a bad dude Angel is. He's serving the soup in the Dining Hall tonight. So guess what he says to me? He says, 'Bernie, I hate carrying that big soup pot around. I get so totally nervous. I hope I don't spill any on you.'"

My two buddies stared at me. Feenman shrugged. "So?"

"Don't you see what he was saying?" I cried. "He was getting me ready. Tonight at dinner he's going to pretend to trip. And he's going to spill hot soup all over me."

Crench grabbed my shoulder. "Bernie, that's crazy talk," he said.

"No, it isn't," I insisted. "Then Angel will act really sorry and pretend it was a terrible accident. I'll be covered in hot soup. But he'll get everyone feeling sorry for HIM!"

"Bernie, he'd never do that," Crench said. "You're making this all up."

Feenman painted a third nostril on I. B. Rotten's nose. "You've gotta lighten up about Angel," he said. "You're totally losing it."

"You'll see," I said. "You'll see tonight at dinner."

I was going to wear a rain slicker to dinner. That would spoil Angel's plan. But I decided against it. I wanted everyone in school to see what a bad dude he was.

The Dining Hall is a huge room with three long tables—one for each dorm. I took my seat at the Rotten House table. I didn't eat. I kept my eyes on Angel.

He walked up and down, ladling out soup from an enormous pot. The pot was almost as big as Angel. But he was doing a perfect job.

I knew he was getting ready for me. Getting ready for the "accident" that would cover me in soup.

"May I sit here?"

I heard a voice at my side. I turned to see Mrs. Heinie squinting at me through her thick glasses. "Is this seat empty?" She sat down. She picked up her soup spoon. "I hear that Chef Baloney's pea soup is to die for!" she said.

"Yeah. *I'm* the one who will be dying," I muttered. "You watch, Mrs. Heinie. I know you think

Angel is an angel. But just watch."

"Watch what?" she asked.

Angel was making his way down our table. Closer ... closer ...

"He's gonna pretend to trip, and he'll pour hot pea soup all over me," I said. "Just watch. Maybe you'll change your mind about Angel."

"Bernie, that's crazy!" she said. "Totally crazy."

"Here he comes," I said. "Just watch...."

Chapter 18

SPLOOOOSH! PLOPPPPP!

Angel held the big pot in front of him. I could see the pea soup inside it, boiling hot, thick and lumpy and bright green.

He ladled out a big bowl for Feenman. Then he served soup to Crench and Belzer. But I could see he had his eyes on me.

"Here it comes," I said through gritted teeth.

Angel moved up behind me. He dipped the ladle into the big, steaming pot. He took a step . . . then another.

Whoa. Wait!

He didn't trip. He didn't do it. I knew he planned to fake a fall. I knew he planned to pour the soup over me. But he didn't do it.

He raised the ladle.

He was trying to trick me.

I couldn't let him get away with it. Not with everyone watching.

I stuck my foot out.

"HEY!" Angel let out a startled cry. He stumbled over my shoe.

The pea soup flew from the pot in a steaming, green tidal wave.

I ducked.

I heard a loud splash.

SPLOOOOSH.

Then I heard a wet

PLOPPPPP.

Then I heard Mrs. Heinie's scream.

"YAAAAAIIIII!"

I whipped around and saw the pea soup oozing

down her hair, her face, her dress.

I picked some chunks from her hair. "I told you!" I said. "See? I told you!"

Mrs. Heinie jumped to her feet. She pulled off her glasses. Then she tried to wipe the thick, green gunk off them. "Bernie, you—you—you TRIPPED Angel!" she sputtered. "I saw you!"

"Huh? No way!" I said. "It was all his plan. He told me he was gonna trip and spill the soup. By the way, Mrs. H., you look *great* in green. It's really your color."

"Shut your fat gob," she replied. She wiped thick pea gunk off her neck and shoulders. "I saw you trip him," she said.

"I'm so sorry!" Angel cried. He still held the pot in front of him. "It wasn't Bernie's fault. Don't blame him. I'm just so clumsy. I'll never forgive myself."

He started to bang his head against the side of the soup pot. "I was bad! I was bad! I was BAD!" he chanted.

Through the pea soup, Mrs. Heinie smiled at Angel. "He's so sweet. He's trying to protect you,

Bernie. But it won't work. I saw you trip him."

She grabbed my hand. "Let's have a talk with Headmaster Upchuck. "Let's GO!" she said, pulling me away.

"Go?" I said. "But I didn't get my soup!"

Chapter 19

HIGH-STAKES UNO

"Upchuck gave me one more chance," I told Feenman and Crench later that night. "Just in case it really was an accident."

"Now what are you going to do?" Feenman asked. "Are you going to give Angel a break?" He bit off a big chunk of Nutty Nutty Bar. They were both chomping on candy bars.

"Where'd you get those?" I asked.

CHOMP, CHOMP, CHOMP. "Angel is giving them away again," Feenman said. "What an awesome dude!"

I stomped back to my room and dropped down onto my pitiful cot. I felt so angry, steam poured from my ears. My head was ticking, like a time bomb ready to explode.

I was about to get kicked out of school, thanks to Angel. And now he ruled Rotten House. The whole Rotten SCHOOL.

Everyone loved him. Even my best friends. No one believed that he was a bad dude.

I shut my eyes and tried to think.

How could I make Mrs. Heinie believe me about Angel?

Well . . . what if she caught Angel doing something really bad?

Hmmm . . . *Think, Big B. Think. . . .*

Suddenly, I had a new plan. A better plan!

I remembered . . . tomorrow night . . . Sherman Oaks was having a high-stakes Uno game. No one could get into the game for less than ten dollars a round.

What if Mrs. Heinie caught Angel gambling?

If she caught Angel sneaking out after Lights Out and gambling at Uno, then she'd know he wasn't an angel!

Yes! I'll bring Angel to the game. He'll want to show off to the other guys. He thinks he's *king* of the school now.

And I'll make sure Mrs. Heinie catches him with a big stack of ten-dollar bills.

Perfect.

No. Wait.

Not perfect.

The Bernie B. brain was still chugging.

I had a better plan. Yes. MUCH better.

"I'm taking Angel to the Uno game tomorrow night after Lights Out," I told Feenman.

He stared at me. "You're gonna get him into big trouble so he'll be kicked out of school?"

I shook my head. "No way. Would I do that to him? I'm gonna get ME into big trouble!"

His mouth dropped open. "But if *you* get into big trouble, how will that help you get rid of Angel?"

I patted him on the shoulder. "You'll see," I said. "You'll see...."

Chapter 20

TELL ME ANOTHER ONE

"This is so totally awesome!" Angel whispered. "I've never played cards before. Bernie, you'll have to show me which end to hold."

"No problem," I whispered back.

Like I believed him. Hah.

"You'll probably win a hundred dollars," I said, leading him across the grass. "You'll clean us all out."

He laughed. "I just want to play for the *fun* of it. Not for the money."

Tell me another one, Angel. Wow. This guy could lie!

A bright half-moon shone down on us. It was nearly midnight. The trees were still. The grass glowed with dew.

Sherman Oaks and his pals were waiting behind the Student Center. He had set up a card table and some lights.

Sherman was already shuffling the Uno cards. "Ten dollars," he said, holding out his hand. "It's ten dollars to get into the game."

"This is so totally exciting!" Angel exclaimed. "Look at me. I can barely breathe!"

He took the cards away from Sherman and started shuffling them. "What do you say we make twos and threes wild and jokers high?" he said.

I started to get the idea that maybe Angel had played cards before.

Guess what? He won the first hand. And the second hand. After about an hour he had a big stack of ten-dollar bills on the table.

"Beginner's luck," he said. "That's all it is. Just beginner's luck." He shuffled the Uno cards again.

Time to get down to business. I slipped away and

called Mrs. Heinie on my cell phone. I disguised my voice. I told her I was a concerned citizen. I said there was a card game going on behind the Student Center.

Then I went back to the game. *This isn't gonna be pretty*, I told myself.

Mrs. Heinie came bursting up to us just as Angel won yet again. This time she let out a *HUMPH* that nearly blew over the card table.

"Angel! I'm SHOCKED at you!" she screamed. "I-I-I can't *believe* YOU'RE here after Lights Out, gambling with these boys!"

Angel's mouth dropped open. "Huh? Gambling? Bernie told me they were raising money for the animal shelter in town!"

Good one, huh?

Mrs. Heinie spun around to me. "Bernie, I *knew* you were at fault! Angel was a good boy until he met *you!* Look what you've done to him."

She narrowed her eyes at me. She bit her bottom lip. I could see she was thinking hard.

Finally she said, "I'm sorry, Bernie. I have no choice. I can't let this continue."

I lowered my head. "What are you going to do to me? Kick me out of school? Send me home?"

"Of course not," Mrs. Heinie replied. "I'm going to get Angel his *own* room—as far away from *you* as possible!"

Yesssssssssssssssss!

"No—please!" I pretended to beg. "Please don't take Angel away. I have *big plans* for him! I have plenty *more* things I want to teach him."

"No way," Mrs. Heinie said. "Angel is not going to have any more to do with you, Bernie. You'll never even see him!"

Yesssssssssssssssss!

"Please don't take him away," I said. "I *love* sharing my room with him. I want to teach him *all* my secrets."

"HUMPH!" She grabbed Angel by the shoulders and pushed him away. Angel hurried back to grab the big stack of money he'd won. Then he hurried off with her.

I waited till they disappeared into the darkness. Then I leaped onto Feenman's shoulders and started to celebrate.

My room was mine again. My LIFE was mine again. And it was so *easy*—easy if you're a GENIUS!

Was I happy?

Does a bear eat potato chips in the woods?

I cheered. I shouted. I sang! I let Feenman carry me around for hours!

All my friends came out to celebrate with me. And they were MY friends again! I even let Gassy and Lippy out. Why shouldn't my sweet pets celebrate, too?

And then I brought out a huge bag of Nutty Nutty Bars. "For *everyone!*" I shouted, holding up the chewy, nutty treats.

"Huh? Bernie?" Feenman said. "You mean they're *free?*"

I stared at him. "You're kidding—right?" I handed him a candy bar. "But since it's a party," I said, "they're only a dollar each!"

HERE'S A SNEAK PEEK AT BOOK #11

R.L. STINE'S

ROTTEN SCHOOL

Punk'd
and
Skunked

DATE   SCENE   TAKE

HOW DO
YOU SPELL $$$$?

Beast started chewing the couch cushion again. It was a problem—because three guys were *sitting* on the couch.

"Listen up, dudes," I said. "Haven't you heard about the National School Make-a-Great-Invention Contest?"

They stared at me.

"All three dorms at Rotten School have to make a great invention," I explained. "The winner goes to Preppy Prep Prep to compete with five other schools."

"Is there a prize or something?" Crench asked.

"You *bet* there's a prize," I said. "The winning inventors get *five thousand dollars* in cash. Did you hear me? Cash. That's spelled $$$$! And, you also get to be on TV on MTV-6."

"Wow!"

"Awesome!"

"Totally rad!"

"No way!"

"That got 'em excited. MTV-6 is the best MTV channel of all. They don't play music videos, and they don't talk about anything. They just mess around all day, looking cool.

"We're gonna be on TV and win HUGE bucks," I said, rubbing my hands together. "And, we'll stay at Preppy Prep Prep and live like spoiled rich kids for a whole week!"

I finally got them totally worked up. They began to chant, "Bernie! Bernie! Bernie!" And they picked me up and carried me on their shoulders around the room five or six times.

Finally, I got dizzy and had to hop down.

I raised my fist in the air. "On to Preppy Prep Prep!" I shouted.

"We RULE! Rotten House RULES! YAAAAAAY!"

"Bernie?" a tiny voice whispered.

I turned to see Chipmunk, the shyest kid at Rotten School. He was wedged in the corner. He had his hands covering his face. That's just how shy he is. "Bernie, we have a small problem," he muttered into his hands.

"Problem?" I said. "What kind of problem?"

"We don't have an invention."

ABOUT the AUTHOR

R.L. Stine graduated from Rotten School with a solid D+ average, which put him at the top of his class. He says that his favorite activities at school were Scratching Body Parts and Making Armpit Noises.

In sixth grade, R.L. won the school Athletic Award for his performance in the Wedgie Championships. Unfortunately, after the tournament, his underpants had to be surgically removed.

After graduation, R.L. became well known for writing scary book series such as The Nightmare Room, Fear Street, Goosebumps, and Mostly Ghostly, and a short story collection called *Beware!*

Today, R.L. lives in New York City, where he is busy writing stories about his school days.

For more information about R.L. Stine,
go to www.rottenschool.com
and www.rlstine.com